I'll Share With You

by Linda Apolzon
illustrated by Kathy Wilburn

A GOLDEN BOOK • NEW YORK

Western Publishing Company, Inc., Racine, Wisconsin 53404

© 1986 by Linda Apolzon. Illustrations © 1986 by Kathy Wilburn. All rights reserved. Printed in the U.S.A. GOLDEN®, GOLDEN & DESIGN®, and A FIRST LITTLE GOLDEN BOOK® are trademarks of Western Publishing Company, Inc. No part of this book may be reproduced or copied in any form without written permission from the publisher. Library of Congress Catalog Card Number: 85-81566 ISBN 0-307-10166-5
ABCDEFGHIJ

Kelly and Carl are sister and brother. Every morning they play outside. Carl shares his wagon with Kelly. They push the wagon to the top of the hill.

Carl and Kelly climb in. They hold on to the sides. The wagon rolls down the hill. *Bumpity! Bumpity!*

On the tree is a swing. Today Mommy pushes Kelly first. *Swoosh!* Kelly swoops through the air.

After a while Mommy says, "Now it's Carl's turn." Slower and slower Kelly swings until she stops.

Carl jumps onto the swing with a happy face.

After a while Carl asks if he can paint the garage. Mommy gives him a pail of water and a big paintbrush. Carl dips the brush into the water. He slaps it against the garage.

"I want to paint, too," says Kelly.

But there is only one brush. Kelly has to wait.

When it is Kelly's turn, she paints the back steps.

Then it is time for lunch and a nap.

After her nap, Kelly plays with her tea set. Carl picks up a teacup and pretends to feed the baby doll.

"That's my baby!" Kelly says.

She snatches at the cup. It flies across the table and clatters to the floor. Carl kicks a chair over, and Kelly screams.

Mommy comes in. She tells Kelly, "If you won't share your tea set, then you'll have to be alone."

Mommy takes Carl out of the room.

Kelly puts her dishes just the way she
wants them. The room is very quiet.
Kelly feels sad.

"Mommy!" she calls. "Can Carl come back now?"

"Yes, he may," Mommy answers.

Carl comes back into the room. "I'll share with you," Kelly says. "You can be the baby's father."

"O.K.," says Carl.

Kelly and Carl pretend it is the doll's birthday. They give her a purple cake with pink frosting. A clown comes to the party and brings a baby elephant.

Later, Daddy reads Kelly a goodnight story.
She can hear Carl and Mommy reading and
laughing in Carl's room.

"Sleep well!" Daddy whispers, and tucks
her in.

Tomorrow Kelly will share with Carl again.
Carl is Kelly's best friend.